FOR LUCIE

MILET PUBLISHING LTD
6 NORTH END PARADE
LONDON W14 0SJ
ENGLAND
EMAIL info@milet.com
WEB SITE www.milet.com

PINK LEMON

ISBN 1 84059 330 X

PRINTED IN CHINA

HERVÉ TULLET

PINK
LEMON

MILET

PINK

LEMON?

RED

SNOW?

BROWN

PEAS ?

YELLOW FIRE ENGINE?

BLUE BEARD?

HAIR?

YELLOW

SEA?

WHITE

SANTA

CLAUS ?

YELLOW

GHOST?

PURPLE

LADYBIRD ?

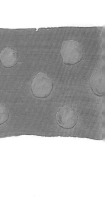

CHRISTMAS

TREE ?

RED
EGG?

BLUE

TRAFFIC LIGHT?

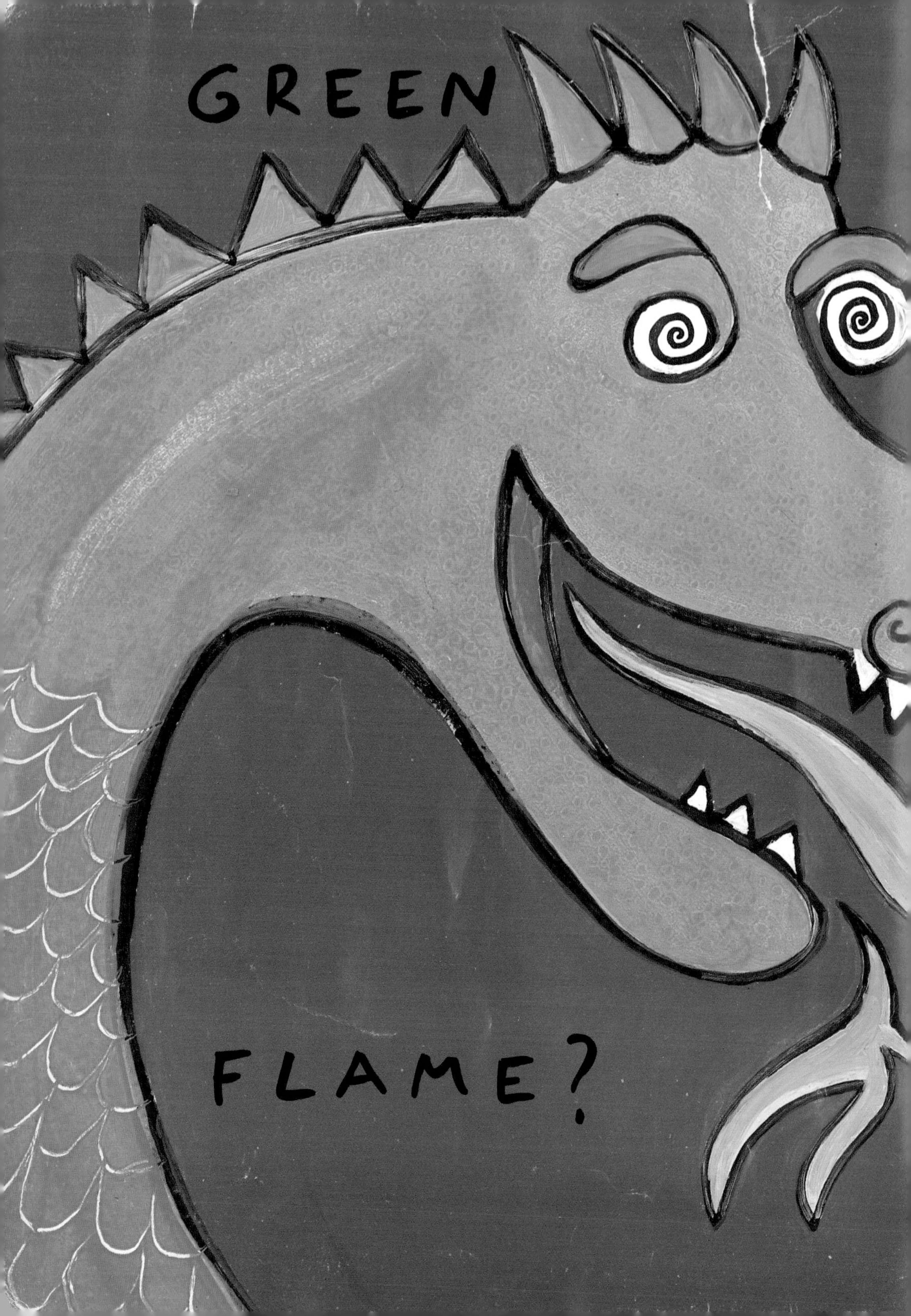
GREEN
FLAME?

GREEN

SUN ?

ORANGE

SHARK?

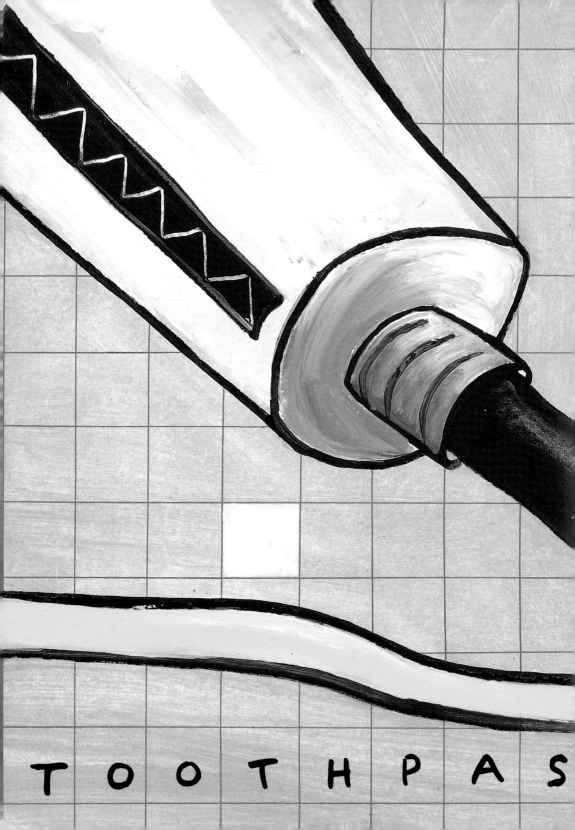

TOOTHPAS

YELLOW

BLUE
CARDS ?

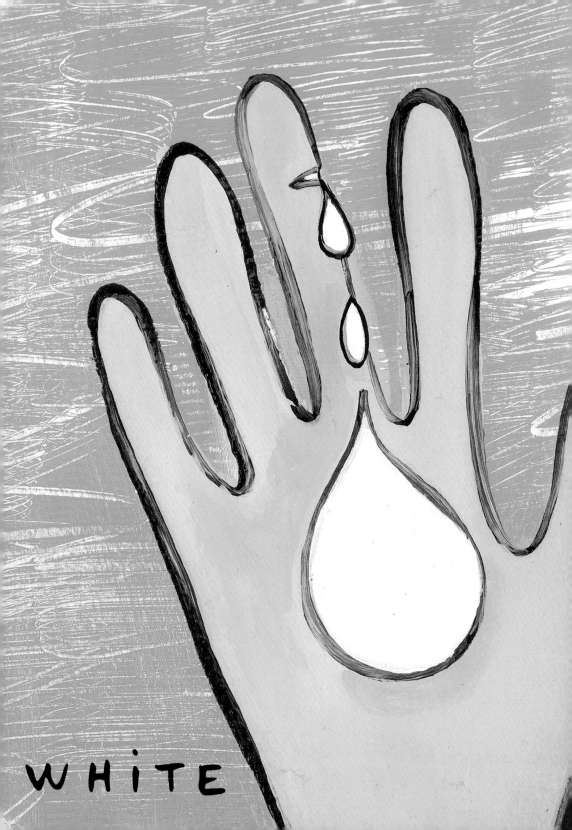

WHITE

BLOOD?

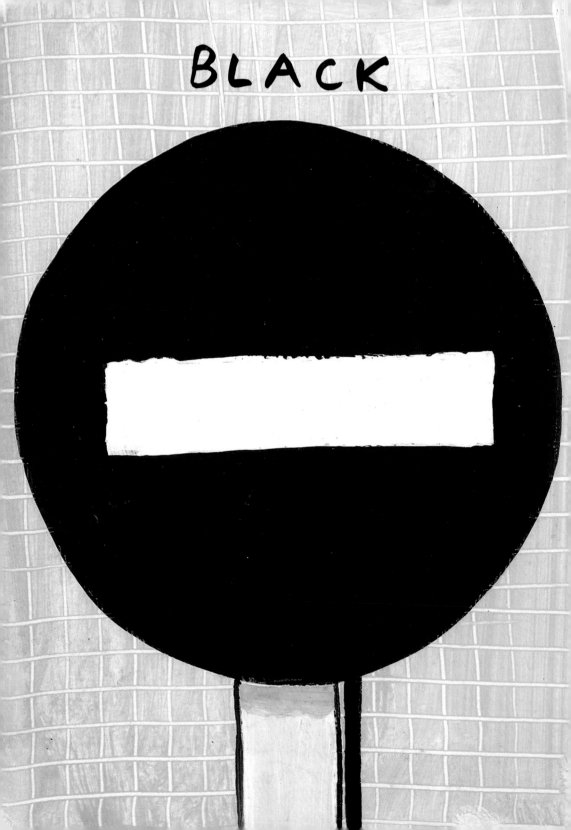

ROAD

SiGN ?

RED

FRiES?

APPLE ?

DALMA

YELLOW

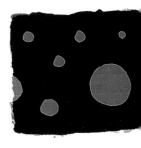

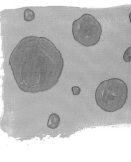

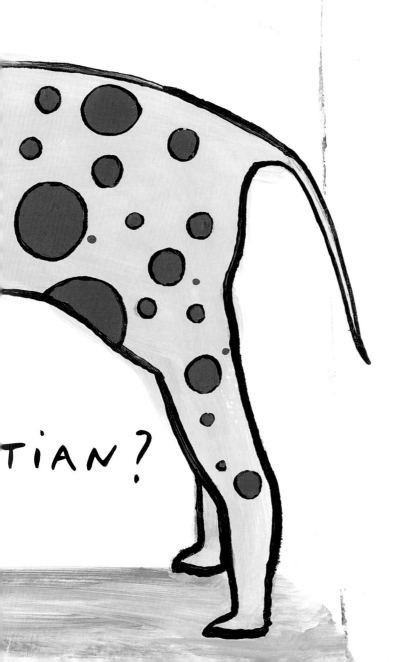

TIAN?

BLUE

MUSHROOMS?

BROWN

CLOUDS?

PINK

DOVE?

S K E L E T O N ?

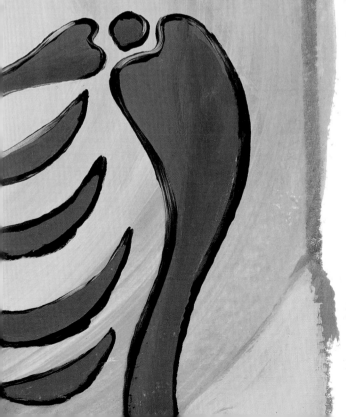

MOON?

RAIN?

RED

SAND ?

WHITE

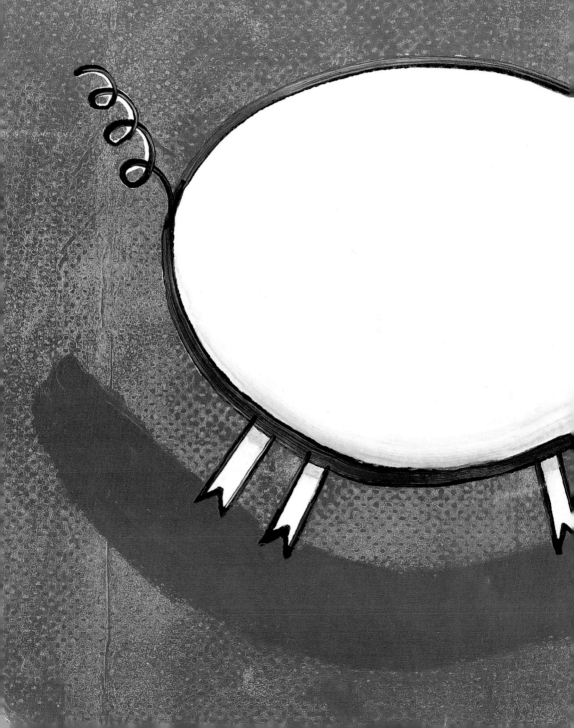

PiG ?

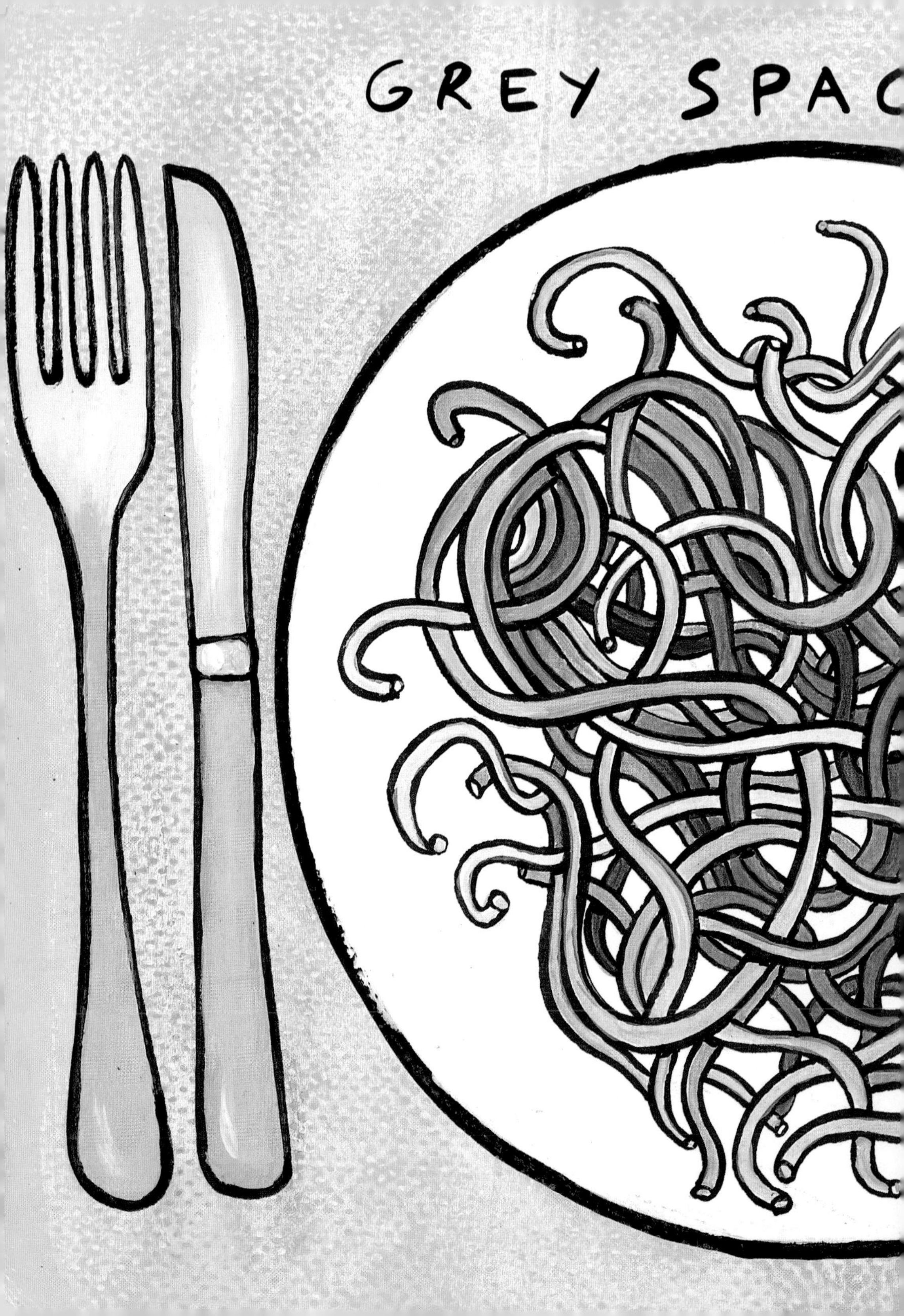
GREY SPAC

ETTi ?

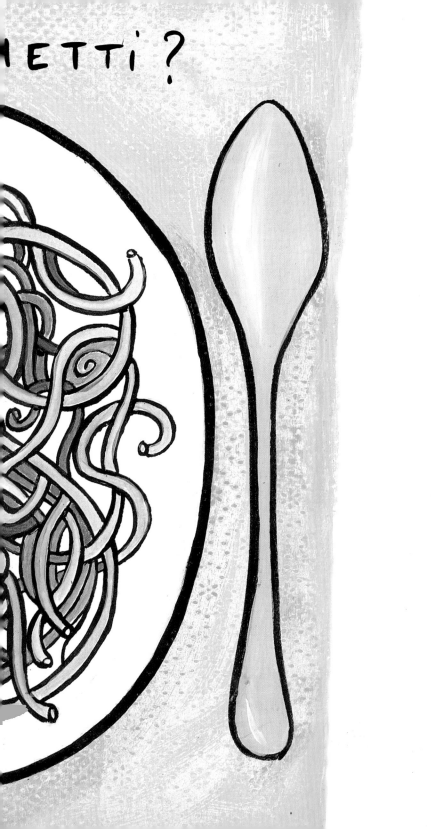

GREEN

MOUSE ?

BROWN

CHEESE ?

GREY

ROSE?

PURPLE

BEE?

PINK

SPIDER?

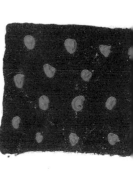

ORANGE

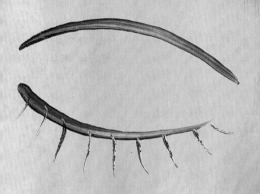

TEARS?

ORANGE?

GREEN

MILK?

ORANGE

MARTiAN?

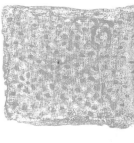